This ~~treasure~~ book
belongs to:
....

COOKIES

COOKIES

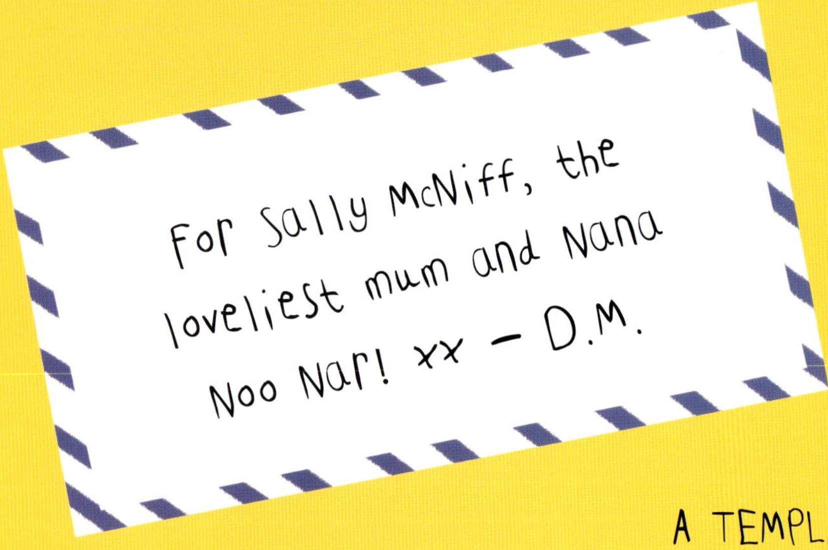

A TEMPLAR BOOK

First published in the UK in 2025 by Templar Books,
an imprint of Bonnier Books UK
5th Floor, HYLO,
105 Bunhill Row, London, EC1Y 8LZ
The authorised representative in the EEA is Bonnier Books UK (Ireland) Limited.
Registered office address:
Floor 3, Block 3, Miesian Plaza, Dublin 2, D02 Y754, Ireland
compliance@bonnierbooks.ie

1 3 5 7 9 10 8 6 4 2

055 0425

ISBN 978-1-80078-454-3

This book was typeset in Childs Play Age Eight, Natural Blues, Meowtalk and Snacky Plop.
The illustrations were created digitally, with a little help from Leo and Finn.

Edited by Ruth Symons and Amelia Warren
Designed by Laura Hall
Production by Neil Randles and Nick Read

Printed in China

JAY RUNS AWAY

DAWN McNIFF

NICOLA SLATER

templar books

PARROTS of the WORLD

go PIRATES!
PIRATE CAPTAIN
WANTS YOU
TO JOIN THE HIGH SEAS
BABY GIRL
Dare ye enter!

NO BABIES
KEEP OUT

PELICAN
POST

Mister Pirate Captain
The Far Away Ocean
Very Far Away
PELICAN
POST

XXX

Dear Jay

No problem – I'll send my pirate crew to fetch you now. I'm making you Head of Parrots.

Welcome to the glorious life on the ocean wave!

Regards

The Captain

Dear Mum and Dad
You probably haven't noticed that I've gone (because you're so busy playing with Flossie ALL THE TIME), but I've left to join the pirates.
So, GOODBYE!
Love from
Jay the Pirate
Head of Parrots

Dearest Jay
Please come home.
We miss you and love you.
And so does Flossie.
lots of love
Mum and Dad xxx

A PIRATE'S LIFE FOR ME!
Wish you were here!
MUM

MUM

In case you don't believe that I'm happy, here are the photos as proof! Just look...

Me having fun without you on an actual, REAL-LIFE pirate ship, looking after LOADS of pretty parrots!

Me being allowed to eat ship biscuits for breakfast, lunch AND tea!

Me with Mister Pirate Captain – my new, cool dad, who has ZERO babies!

(He can be a bit grumpy, but it's fine...)

I probably won't write for a while now because I'm far too busy and important doing pirate things.

(And anyway, I've run out of stamps.)

Jay

NO AIRMAIL
DUE TO
BAD WEATHER
PELICAN
POST

Jay
Head of Parrots
Bellychurn Galleon
The Far Away Ocean
BCI VOM
10

Dear Mum and Dad

I got your last letter, thank you. It's been... okay here. I'm sending some more photos...

Me in my bedroom, that I DON'T have to share!

It is quite small. And high. And completely freezing. But it's fine.

Me with my NOT-BORING shipmate family.

They do play quite rough games, but it's fine.

Me eating more biscuits.

Some have worms in them, but it's fine.

Me with more parrots...

They're noisier than Flossie, if you can imagine that. And they do a LOT of poo – they could do with some nappies! But it's fine.

Me still living a glorious life on the ocean wave.

I do get a bit seasick, but it's fine.

P.S. Do you think you could send me my old teddy?

And maybe a recording of Dad reading a bedtime story?

And perhaps some cabbage or something – just to make a change from the biscuits?

By the way, how are things there...?

Jay x

PELICAN POST
LARGE PACKAGES incur a cost of 3 HERRINGS
JAY

JAY

RAISINS

Dear Mum and Dad...
and Flossie

Thanks for the parcel. The cabbage was actually really yummy...

I found this ball floating out at sea. I thought Flossie might like it, so I'm sending it to you. I don't mind if she doesn't. Whatever.

Love

Jay x

Dear Jay
Flossie loved the ball! She doesn't have anyone to play with though...
love
Mum and Dad xxx
Jay
Head of Parrots
Bellychurn Galleon
The Far Away Ocean
BC1 VOM

DROPPING JOURNEY
YE BO

ELICAN
POST

Dear Mister Pirate Captain
I'm sorry, but I have to resign as Head of Parrots.
It turns out that life on the ocean wave isn't for me. And besides, Flossie really needs me here for snuggling and footie practice.
Thanks for everything.
Love
Jay x
P.S. I've also included your invitation to my PIRATE birthday party. Please come!

Ahoy, me fellow readers!
Epic adventure, right?

If you fancy a quest across the high seas, write a letter to Mister Pirate Captain!

Let him know where you'd like to go, what you'd like to see and who will be going with you (so he can make sure there are enough hammocks).

Yo Ho Ho!
Happy sailing!

I've included the ship's address for you – it can be tricky to track down!

Here's a stamp for your letter – Pelican Post deliver, come rain or shine!

Draw some pictures of your adventures here!

P.S. If you'd like to write a longer letter, you can create your own parchment using a piece of paper and a cold, wet tea bag!